The Sleepover Club

Have you been
invited to all these
sleepovers?

The Sleepover Club at Frankie's
The Sleepover Club at Lyndsey's
The Sleepover Club at Felicity's
The Sleepover Club at Rosie's
The Sleepover Club at Kenny's
Starring the Sleepover Club
The Sleepover Girls go Spice
The 24 Hour Sleepover Club
The Sleepover Club Sleeps Out
Happy Birthday, Sleepover Club
Sleepover Girls on Horseback
Sleepover in Spain
Sleepover on Friday 13th
Sleepover Girls at Camp
Sleepover Girls go Detective
Sleepover Girls go Designer

The Sleepover Club
Surfs the Net

by Fiona Cummings

Collins

An imprint of HarperCollins*Publishers*

The Sleepover Club ® is a Registered Trademark
of HarperCollins*Publishers* Ltd

First published in Great Britain by Collins in 1999
Collins is an imprint of HarperCollins*Publishers* Ltd,
77-85 Fulham Palace Road, Hammersmith,
London W6 8JB

The HarperCollins website address is
www.**fire**and**water**.com

5 7 9 11 13 12 10 8 6

Text copyright © Fiona Cummings 1999

Original series characters, plotlines
and settings © Rose Impey 1997

ISBN 0 00 675445 7

The author asserts the moral right to
be identified as the author of the work.

Printed and bound in England by
Clays Ltd, St Ives plc

Sleepover Kit List

1. Sleeping bag
2. Pillow
3. Pyjamas or a nightdress
4. Slippers
5. Toothbrush, toothpaste, soap etc
6. Towel
7. Teddy
8. A creepy story
9. Food for a midnight feast:
   chocolate, crisps, sweets, biscuits.
   In fact anything you like to eat.
10. Torch
11. Hairbrush
12. Hair things like a bobble or hairband,
    if you need them
13. Clean knickers and socks
14. Change of clothes for the next day
15. Sleepover diary and membership card

CHAPTER ONE

Hi there. It's good to see you again. You're actually the first one here, but that's cool. Rosie has just rung to say that she'll be along as soon as her mum gets home. Kenny's running late, playing football I expect, and Lyndz is probably still at the stables with her precious horses. Fliss is coming straight from her dad's and she finds it really hard tearing herself away from his baby, Posie. But hey, I can understand that. I'm going to be like that myself in seven months' time. I *can't wait* until Mum has her baby. I'd pestered her to have a baby for ages. She used to roll her eyes and say, "Oh no Frankie, not again!" So hearing that she was pregnant was the best news *ever*.

Anyway, come on in. We can go up to my room while we wait for the others. They shouldn't be too long. And it'll give me a chance to fill you in on the latest news. *And* you can have a go on the Internet in peace. You won't get a look in when the others get here, believe me!

I don't know how much you know about the Internet, but it's totally cool. When I heard Mum and Dad talking about it at first though, it all sounded a bit weird.

"Isn't it a bit nerdy?" I asked Dad doubtfully.

"Nerdy?" asked Dad, pretending to sound shocked. "This is communication for the future, young lady, and you'd better get used to it!"

I still wasn't convinced. I mean, computers are boring, aren't they? I'd heard a couple of kids at school going on about the Internet, but it never really sank in, to be honest. It was only when Mum became pregnant that it became an issue at home. You see, she's kind of old to be having a second baby and Dad wanted her to take things a bit easier, so she's started working from home a couple of days a week. She's a lawyer and needs to keep up with other cases. And how can you do that? You've guessed it – on the Internet!

So, one minute we had a perfectly ordinary computer, and the next we were hooked up to the Net. Dad spent ages fiddling about on it, so I went to see what he was doing. He tapped in a kind of code, and he seemed to be able to get any information that he wanted.

"I don't understand," I told him after a while. "How come our computer knows so much stuff all of a sudden?"

"Because our little computer is now hooked up to a huge network of lots of other computers," he explained. "From computers in someone's home to vast computers owned by some of the world's biggest organisations. So when you go on to the Internet, you really do have the world at your fingertips! Why don't you have a go?"

Dad showed me which keys to press, and it was totally amazing. I mean, you really can find out everything – from the colour of Ronan

Keating's underpants to the temperature at the top of Mount Everest!

"You're a real surfer now," Dad laughed.

"What do you mean?" I asked, all confused. When had we started talking about the sea?

"When you move around web sites searching for information, it's called 'surfing the Net'!" Dad explained.

"Cool!" I'd always liked the sound of surfing, and this way I didn't even have to get wet!

"And I know how much you like spiders…!" said Dad, walking his fingers up my arm like some massive creepy-crawly.

"Get off!" I screamed. "I *hate* spiders. What have they got to do with the Internet?"

"Absolutely nothing!" grinned Dad. "But you often hear the word 'web' associated with the Internet. People talk about the 'World Wide Web'. I know it sounds more like something created by a tarantula the size of Godzilla…"

"Eeeuuuurgh!" I screeched, and pretended to faint really dramatically.

"It may be a weird name," laughed Dad,

"but it's just a way of storing and getting into all the information on the Internet."

"Oh right. But why couldn't we have the Internet before?" I asked.

"Because to access it, our computer needed a special modem," Dad explained. "And it all works through the telephone system, which is pretty amazing really."

I think Dad could sense that my eyes were glazing over a bit at that point, because then he said hurriedly, "That's all you really need to know. Why don't you just play around with it for a while?"

And I did – for hours and hours. He virtually had to drag me off in the end. There's so much information on the Internet. And the great thing is that when you get bored looking at one thing, then it's easy to look up something else! It's just so great!

I hadn't mentioned it to my friends before, because, as I said, I wasn't *that* excited till Dad explained it. But once I'd got the hang of it, well that was a different story. I was dying to tell *everyone* about it.

In the playground the next day, I leapt on Fliss as soon as she came through the gates.

"Hey Fliss, you'll never guess what happened last night!" I screamed.

"Oh Frankie, I *hate* it when you say that. Millions of things could have happened," she sighed. "And you only make fun of me when I try to guess."

"You were visited by aliens?" suggested Rosie, who had crept up behind me.

"We're not playing one of her stupid guessing games, are we?" asked Kenny, flinging her bag to the ground. "OK, you scored the winning goal for Leicester City. She shoots! She scores! YEAAH!" She started running around like a demented chicken. I don't need to remind you, do I, that Kenny is obsessed with football.

"No, you'll never guess!" I squealed. "Dad's only got us hooked up, hasn't he?"

The others were looking at me blankly.

"You know – we're on the Net."

Still no response.

"We're on the *Internet*, you dummies," I told

them. "Crikey, don't all get excited at once, will you?"

Kenny and Fliss *still* looked totally blank, but Rosie had suddenly come to life.

"Wow! Adam is going to be so jealous when I tell him. He's desperate to use the Internet!"

You remember Adam don't you? He's Rosie's older brother who has cerebral palsy, and he's a total computer freak.

Now Lyndz had appeared too. She's always late, that girl.

"Who's on the Net then?" she asked.

I beamed at her by way of an answer.

"You lucky thing, Frankie!" she grinned. "My brother Stuart's always going on about how great it is. Our grandparents in Holland use it a lot. It sounds brill!"

Kenny and Fliss were still looking pretty confused, so we had to try to explain to them what the Internet was all about. But Fliss just couldn't get her head round it.

"You mean that all the computers in the world can talk to each other? I didn't think they could do that." She pulled a dramatic face. "I mean, that is really *spooky*."

Before I could explain it to her again, the bell went. We shuffled like penguins into the classroom. We often do stuff like that. Everybody seems to think we're crazy – I don't know why!

Sometimes school can be really boring. Mrs Weaver tries her best, but let's face it – the only way Maths could get exciting is if Boyzone and 911 got together to demonstrate the complicated bits. And somehow I don't think that's ever going to happen. I love doing project work though, and that particular week we were in the middle of learning all about the Vikings.

"Wouldn't it be great if instead of just reading about them, we could actually *see* a proper Viking and ask him about his life? What he ate, what he wore, stuff like that," said Rosie, looking up from her work.

"That would be so cool!" I agreed.

"Actually, there's a place called the Yorvik Centre in York which does just that," said Mrs

14

Weaver, who had suddenly appeared from nowhere. "People dressed as Vikings show you round the exhibition and tell you all about their way of life 1,000 years ago. It's a pity that it's just a little too far away for us to visit."

"That's too bad," agreed Kenny. "We'll just have to make do with boring books then!"

Mrs Weaver flashed one of her 'You're-very-lucky-to-have-so-many-lovely-books-at-school' looks and went to see what the M&Ms, Emma Hughes and Emily Berryman, were up to. You remember the deadly duo, don't you? Well they were in full-on smarming mode. It turned out that they'd both been to the Yorvik Centre, so they managed to suck up to Mrs Weaver big time. That was when Kenny was struck by inspiration.

"I bet you've found loads of stuff about Vikings on the Internet, haven't you Frankie?" she asked me in a really loud voice, as though I was deaf or something.

"I…I…I don't…" I stuttered, all confused. Then I realised what she was doing. "Oh yes, there are *loads* of web sites about Vikings!"

I replied, louder still.

"And I bet they're really exciting too, aren't they?" Lyndz chimed in.

"Ooh yes," I said enthusiastically. "They've just got so much, er, so much… stuff on them!"

"Stuff?" Kenny mouthed to me. "Couldn't you think of anything more exciting?"

I just shrugged.

"Well Francesca, I'm all for using new technology," Mrs Weaver smiled. "Maybe you can look up Vikings on the Internet again and report back to us on all the exciting 'stuff' that you find."

The M&Ms sniggered, but I could tell that they were really peeved. They're always the centre of attention, those two. It was nice to feel a bit special for once.

"Hey, nice one Frankie!" laughed Kenny. "So when can we come round to your place to do a bit of surfing?"

Poor Fliss looked absolutely panic-stricken.

"The sooner we get Fliss used to the Internet, the better," I decided. "I'll ask Mum and Dad tonight, but I'm sure it'll be fine if you come home with me after school tomorrow!"

Little did I know then what chaos the Internet was going to lead me into…

CHAPTER TWO

The next day was one of Mum's days for working at home, so it was no problem for the others to come back with me after school. As soon as I opened the front door, my dog Pepsi leapt at me. She is one crazy dog!

"What a welcome!" laughed Mum, making a grab for her collar. "Now calm down Pepsi, these girls need to save their strength for tackling the 'Information Superhighway'!"

The others looked at her like she was talking a foreign language.

"She's talking about us using the Internet," I explained.

"That's right girls, you're going to need a

whole new vocabulary from now on," Mum nodded. "It's hi-tech stuff you know, floating around in cyberspace. You'd better make sure that you don't get lost, Fliss!"

Fliss looked terrified.

"Don't be mean, Mother!" I said. "It's OK Fliss, it's all perfectly safe, honest!"

Fliss gave a strained sort of smile. I swear that she takes her sense of humour off with her clothes at night, and sometimes forgets to put it back on again!

"There's Coke and biccies in the kitchen," Mum told us. "Just give me a shout when you're ready and I'll get you set up on your computer."

She disappeared upstairs to her study and we all piled into the kitchen with Pepsi dancing round our ankles.

You wouldn't believe what Kenny did as the rest of us were drinking our Coke. She only shoved *three* Jaffa cakes in her mouth at once, didn't she? After she'd grossed us out with that, it was a relief to get upstairs to the computer!

"OK Mum, you can do your stuff now!" I called.

Before signing on to the Internet, Mum has to type in a special password, which only she and Dad know. They reckon it will stop me using it for hours in the middle of the night – as if! Dad thinks I run up a big enough phone bill as it is, talking to my friends all the time!

Mum sat down at my computer and we all turned round with our backs to her. But I could see Fliss having a sneaky peek at what Mum was typing.

"OK girls, you're logged on now, but don't be on too long, will you?" Mum got up and went back into her study.

I sat down and asked the others which web sites they wanted me to find.

"Will there be anything on Boyzone?" asked Rosie.

"No, Leicester City!" shouted Kenny.

"What about horses?" asked Lyndz.

"I thought we were supposed to be finding out about Vikings!" said Fliss. "Mum told me that this would happen. She said that the

Internet is just a big time-waster. I mean what can it tell you about Boyzone that you can't read in a magazine?"

Sometimes Fliss really annoys me. She was only putting the Internet down because she didn't know anything about it. And I don't suppose her mum did either. I was determined to prove them wrong, so I angrily typed 'Boyzone' in the 'search' box. After a few seconds, a list of web sites devoted to the band popped up. There were loads of them. I pointed the mouse, and clicked on the first one. A picture of Boyzone appeared on the screen. Lots of other boxes surrounded it, so I chose the 'interview' box and then clicked on the 'audio' box next to it. Suddenly the room was filled with their lovely voices.

"Isn't this just great!" I squeaked with excitement.

"It's totally wicked!" giggled Rosie.

"And you certainly don't get *that* in a magazine!" laughed Lyndz.

Fliss looked kind of fascinated, but I knew that she wouldn't say anything. If Fliss has made a stand about something, she doesn't back down easily.

"What about Leicester City now?" Kenny pleaded.

"OK, OK, I'll see what I can do," I said.

Sure enough, there was a web site devoted to Leicester City which Kenny thought was really great. It had a section for young supporters and everything.

It looked as though Kenny was going to hog the computer all night, so I said, "Well I guess we ought to look up those Vikings. We don't want to disappoint Mrs Weaver and the M&Ms now, do we?"

I promised Lyndz that we'd look up horses another time, and typed 'Vikings' into the 'search' box on the screen. I held my breath. I mean, it would be just my luck if I'd been raving to Mrs Weaver about how much information I'd found about Vikings on the Internet, and there really wasn't anything at all. Well, let me tell you – I needn't have worried about that. There were just so many sites about them, we didn't know where to start.

We went into some of the web sites, but we knew that they weren't for us. They looked kind of boring with too many long words and no pictures. Fliss looked very smug when she saw them. But then we hit gold. There was this really brilliant web site that told you loads of stuff about what Vikings ate and wore. But better than that, it also had loads of pictures and – get this – an audio track too. It was like a soundtrack of the stuff Vikings would have heard in their everyday lives. Kind of spooky, huh? Even Fliss had to admit that it was pretty awesome.

"I've got to write some of this stuff down!" shrieked Rosie, reaching for her bag.

"Me too!" yelled Lyndz.

"I'll remember it all, no problem," said Kenny, her eyes glued to the screen. But even she jotted down a few notes when she thought no one was looking.

"Hey you guys," I laughed. "You do realise that we're doing homework without anyone breathing down our necks about it? It's a bit worrying!"

"Maybe the Internet's turning us into little swots!" shrieked Kenny. "Ah no, anything but that!"

She pretended to start shaking. Then, clutching her head, she collapsed on to the floor. That was our cue to dive on top of her and create a human sandwich.

"I thought it was too good to be true!" said Mum, coming into the room. "I knew all that silence couldn't last!"

She went over to the computer and checked that the Internet had switched itself off.

"Well was that any help then?" she asked. "I mean surfing the Net, NOT the human pile-up!"

"Totally!"

"It was *excellent*!"

"So cool!"

"Really brilliant!" That was Fliss. I couldn't help smiling when she said that. *And* it was Fliss who reminded Mrs Weaver the next morning that she'd asked me to report back about Vikings on the Internet.

I explained about the web site and the

noises and everything, and the others chipped in. Before we knew where we were, we'd been talking for about ten minutes. And all the rest of the class seemed to be listening to us too. I'm not sure about the M&Ms though because I didn't look at them. When we'd finished, Mrs Weaver asked everybody to give us a clap.

"Well girls, you've just solved a problem for me. As you know, it's our class assembly next week and we're doing it on the Vikings," Mrs Weaver explained. "I was wondering who should have the major speaking parts. But as you five have shown so much enthusiasm by finding out about the topic yourselves, it seems only fair that you should be the ones to share your knowledge with the rest of the school!"

To be honest, I didn't know what to think about that. I like to feel important, but I'm just not sure whether I like feeling important in front of the whole school. One great thing though was that the M&Ms looked *absolutely furious!*

*   *   *

I don't know what your teacher's like about class assemblies. I know some of them get really wound up, don't they? Well, Mrs Weaver is actually quite cool. She let me, Kenny, Rosie, Lyndz and Fliss help her to write this one. We came up with some really great ideas to use and you could tell that she was dead impressed. The M&Ms were very freaked though. They're so used to being the stars all the time; they couldn't bear us getting all the attention. So of course we milked it for all we were worth! I kept bringing in things that I'd printed from the Viking web sites, and you should have seen their faces – MAD wasn't in it!

We decided that we'd start the assembly with Vikings in a longship ready to land in Britain. We'd show them raiding a village, and then move on to how they lived their lives: the food they ate, the clothes they wore, general things like that. It *seemed* pretty straightforward at the time. But then we hadn't bargained for our dumb classmates, had we?

Everything went really well right up to the day of the performance. I suppose we should have known that it was too good to last.

We'd had a rehearsal where Ryan Scott had got a bit carried away with the oar he was carrying from the pretend longship. He'd poked it up Fliss's dress without her knowing. It was only when everyone started laughing that she realised that her knickers were on show to the whole class. I thought she was going to die of embarrassment. As punishment, Mrs Weaver told Scotty-chops that he couldn't be a Viking any more. Major sulk-fest!

Anyway, on the morning of the assembly we were all really nervous. Me especially, because I had to introduce it to the whole school. I stood up and I could hear my voice trembling. It was awful.

The first thing that went wrong was that the model of the longship fell over. All the boys looked really stupid sitting on the PE benches pretending to row. So, in order to restore their street cred in front of their mates, they went absolutely berserk when they pretended to raid the town. It's a good thing that Mrs Weaver had insisted on using flimsy paper swords or else there would have been blood all over the stage. Ryan Scott was still angry about not being a Viking, so he did his bit as a brave villager trying to prevent their raid. Only he did it a bit too well and refused to surrender. When it looked as though his fight with Danny McCloud was getting out of control, Kenny calmly walked on to the stage and bopped him one. He certainly didn't expect that.

After that, *everything* seemed to go wrong. The M&Ms left grain scattered on the floor after their demonstration of Viking cooking. I'm sure they did that on purpose. Poor Fliss didn't stand a chance when she was doing her supermodel impersonation demonstrating Viking fashion. She skidded and fell right over, taking Lyndz, who was narrating, with her.

By then the whole school was in an uproar, and Mrs Poole the headmistress had to step in to calm things down. It was dead embarrassing and Mrs Weaver looked furious.

"I wish I'd never heard about the stupid Vikings!" I whispered to Kenny as we were making our way back to our classroom.

"You and me both!" agreed Kenny.

"I wish we'd never been on the Internet," hissed Fliss behind us. "If you hadn't swanked about it so much, we wouldn't have been so involved in the assembly in the first place. I'm sure that Mrs Weaver's going to blame us for everything."

Looking at Mrs Weaver's face, I thought that Fliss was probably right.

CHAPTER THREE

We were all really subdued as we trooped back into the classroom. We looked pretty funny still dressed in our Viking costumes, but nobody laughed. Even stupid Ryan Scott, who usually has a joke about everything, was silent.

When Mrs Weaver came in she just sat at her desk for five minutes not saying anything, just staring at us. It was awful. When she finally spoke her voice was very, very quiet, but we knew by the tone of it that she was very, very cross.

"I have been teaching for a very long time," she told us. "And I have never been as ashamed of a class as I was of you just now. I do not expect World War Three to break out when we are trying to present an assembly about the Vikings. And I will not tolerate being made to look a laughing stock in front of the whole school."

Big red blotches had begun to spread on her cheeks. I looked at Kenny and Rosie who both pulled faces at me. Lyndz had her head down and Fliss looked as though she was about to cry.

"I want you to take your maths books out and get on with your work quietly," Mrs Weaver said. "And if I hear one peep out of any of you, I will not be responsible for my actions."

Well, that was the worst morning at school *ever*. It didn't get any better either. At break time we had to put up with stupid kids pointing and laughing at us. But it was worse at lunchtime when the dreaded M&Ms sidled over to us.

"I hope you're happy," hissed Emma Hughes. "It's *your* fault that everything went wrong this morning. If you hadn't been so la-di-da about the stupid Internet, Mrs Weaver would never have let you take over the assembly. Emily and I would have made a much better job of it."

"At least now she knows that you're not capable of doing anything properly," said Emily Berryman in her gruff voice. "And she'll never trust you with anything again!"

Then they both tossed their blonde hair and stalked away.

"They are joking, aren't they?" whispered Fliss. "Mrs Weaver can't treat us like this for ever, can she?"

"It's Ryan Scott she should be cross with, acting like a mad axeman for no reason," said Lyndz. "Although you did flatten him Kenny, which I don't suppose looked very good."

"He deserved it, he was ruining everything," explained Kenny. "I should have flattened those stupid M&Ms as well, for turning the stage into a skating rink."

"Yes, I really hurt myself when I fell," moaned Fliss, rubbing her back.

"None of us came out of it very well, did we?" I asked. "I think we should prove to Mrs Weaver that we do know how to behave properly. Then she just might forget about the assembly."

That afternoon we were extra good. We worked in total silence and we tidied up everywhere without being asked. Mrs Weaver was still angry though and it was a relief when the bell rang for home time.

"Thank goodness that's over!" sighed Rosie. We were just getting all our stuff together when Kenny cartwheeled past us down the playground.

"Phew, that's better!" she said when she was upright again. "I needed that. I'm sure all that keeping quiet isn't good for you!"

Lyndz and Fliss were already at the school gates with Fliss's brother Callum.

"What a bunch of losers!" he laughed when Kenny, Rosie and I joined them. "That assembly was funnier than the stuff you see on the telly. Only it wasn't meant to be, was it? Ha, ha!"

Fliss thumped him hard on his arm. "Shut up Callum!" she yelled.

The walk home was our quietest ever – none of us could bear to speak.

"Best behaviour again tomorrow, OK?" I warned the others as we all said goodbye.

I was so miserable when I got home that I couldn't even talk to Mum and Dad about what had happened.

"Who's that girl sitting on our floor?" whispered Dad loudly to Mum as we were watching television that evening.

"I think it's Francesca, you know, our daughter," Mum replied. "She's usually on the Internet at this time – that's why you don't recognise her!"

"Very funny," I said out loud. "I just thought I'd watch TV with you for a change. That's OK, isn't it?"

They were watching a really boring documentary which I'd never normally watch in a million years. But I couldn't bear to go on the Internet, because for once I thought the M&Ms were right. If I hadn't raved about it so much, we wouldn't have been responsible for our disastrous assembly.

I still felt miserable the next morning. I'd expected the others to feel the same. But when I got into the playground they were acting like mad monkeys, as usual.

"What happened to us being on our best behaviour?" I asked, as I walked up to them.

"Honestly Frankie, you can be so square sometimes!" laughed Kenny. "Lighten up, will you?"

"Look at this, I saw it last night!" Rosie shoved a newspaper cutting under my nose. The headline read:

WIN A COMPUTER AND GET THE INTERNET FREE!

Under-13s design your own Home Page.

Hundreds of prizes up for grabs!

Design a Home Page for a Club or Society to which you belong. The Home Page is the main page of a Club's web site, and should describe the members of the Club and the kind of activities you get up to.

The winning entry will be the one which the judges decide demonstrates the most original and exciting design for a Home Page.

First Prize: A Computer, Internet Package, your Home Page fully designed and accessible on the World Wide Web, plus a selection of 12 CD-Roms.

5 Runners-up Prizes: Your Home Page fully designed and accessible on the World Wide Web, plus a selection of 6 CD-Roms.

Get YOUR Club on the Net NOW!

Well that sounded like a really cool competition. Even if I *had* decided yesterday that the Internet was trouble.

"Well what do you make of that, then?" asked Kenny proudly.

"Yeah, cool!" I said.

"Just imagine actually winning a computer!" giggled Fliss. "I know that you've already got one, but I haven't."

"And what about all those CD-Roms too!" laughed Lyndz. "I love it when we use them at school, but we don't have many, do we? If we won twelve, we'd be able to use them all the time, wouldn't we? On the new computer!"

We all started jumping around really enthusiastically.

"And a Home Page too!" Kenny cried. "Rosie says that if we have our own, people would be able to access it from anywhere in the world, is that right?"

"Yep, I guess so," I nodded, grinning.

Then I stopped jumping around as something occurred to me. "It all sounds great, but I think we're forgetting something," I groaned.

The others all looked at me, and said together, "What?"

"We don't belong to any clubs, do we?" I explained. "What could we have a Home Page of? Mrs Weaver's class at Cuddington Primary School?"

"Nah, that's not very exciting is it? And it's not a club anyway," said Kenny, shaking her head. "What about forming our own five-a-side football team? We'd have a Club to design a Home Page for then."

"No way!" the rest of us shrieked.

"What about writing about horses and the way we saved Mrs McAllister's stables?" asked Lyndz. "That's exciting!"

"Mmm," I agreed. "But that was a one-off thing. It's supposed to be a club we belong to all the time."

The bell went for the start of school.

"Let's think about this and try to sort something out at break time," I told the others. We started to waddle into our classroom like ducks, but we saw Mrs Weaver frowning at us and we remembered that we were supposed to be on our best behaviour.

It was obvious that she was still in a very bad temper when we got into the classroom. It didn't help that we were carrying on with our Viking project. Vikings were bad news for *all* of us. Mrs Weaver said that we had to imagine that we lived in a Viking settlement and describe our daily life. I love writing stories like that. My gran always says that my imagination tends to run away with me anyway.

"And I want no noise please!" Mrs Weaver said sternly.

Kenny and I pulled a face at each other and Fliss started to arrange all her pencils and felt-tips on the table in front of her. She always does that. She's like that at sleepovers too, always very neat and precise with everything. And thinking of that made me realise that we hadn't arranged our next sleepover yet.

'I'll have to call the Sleepover Club together at break,' I thought to myself. Then one of those cartoon light-bulbs went on above my head.

"That's it! I've got it!" I shouted. Unfortunately, I shouted it right out loud!

Everybody turned round to stare at me.

"I do hope that there's a good explanation

for that noise!" said Mrs Weaver sharply, looking up from her desk.

"It was Frankie, Miss," said Emma Hughes. Trust her to drop me right in it.

"And I don't need anyone telling tales, thank you Emma," snapped Mrs Weaver. "Well, Francesca? I'm waiting."

Boy, talk about thinking on your feet. I was red and sweaty and stammering.

"Well, I, erm, I..." Then inspiration struck. "I thought I could write as though I was a Viking child. It'll be a bit, erm, different."

I could hear the M&Ms sniggering.

"That's a very original idea, Francesca, I'll look forward to reading your composition," said Mrs Weaver. "But in future, do you think you could keep your inspiration to yourself? Right, everyone get on. And not another word."

The others were looking at me as though I'd completely lost it.

"I'll tell you at break time," I mouthed to them.

* * *

I couldn't wait for the bell to go. When it did, we all piled out into the playground.

"OK, Frankie, you didn't really get so hyped about your work, did you?" Kenny said. "What's so exciting?"

"I've got it!" I yelled.

"What have you got? Chickenpox?" asked Rosie, innocently.

"No dummy," I laughed. "The club we all belong to. You know, the club for the competition."

"Go on then, spill!" squeaked Fliss.

"*The Sleepover Club*!" I giggled.

"The Sleepover Club! Of course!" yelled Lyndz, leaping up and down. "The most important thing we do, and we almost forgot about it!"

"But is that the kind of club they mean?" asked Fliss.

"It's *exactly* the kind of club which could win us the competition, it's so different," I explained, rolling my eyes a bit. "They said the winner would be the most original entry."

"All right!" yelled Kenny. "Now all we need is

a sleepover, so that we can practise on the Internet and check out lots of other Home Pages."

The others were all looking at me with their dopey, pleading expressions. How could I refuse?

"OK, OK, I'll ask Mum and Dad tonight," I said.

I just hoped that this wasn't going to land us in as much trouble as it had the last time we surfed the Net together. Some hope!

CHAPTER FOUR

Now, as you probably know, my parents are really cool when it comes to letting all my friends come round for sleepovers. They kind of trust me to act sensibly. And although we've done lots of crazy things in our time, we've never done anything *totally* wild. But you know, something strange has happened to my Dad. Ever since he found out that Mum's pregnant, he's been acting kind of weird. He worries that things are going to stress her out and somehow harm the baby. But Mum is just the same as ever – really laid-back about everything. So when I asked Dad about the sleepover, I should have known that it would be a big issue.

"Well, I don't know Frankie," he said, looking all concerned. "You know that your mother needs to take it easy at the moment. And your friends are like the Wild Bunch at the best of times."

"Aw, come on Dad!" I pleaded. "You've never complained before – well, not much. We'll be ever so quiet. We'll be planning our entry for the Internet competition anyway, so we won't be making much noise at all."

"I don't know Frankie," said Dad again, shaking his head. "We've got to be a bit more considerate now, with your mother's condition."

Just at that moment, Mum came into the room.

"What on earth are you talking about, Gwyn? My 'condition' indeed!" she laughed, and playfully slapped Dad's hand. "You make me sound about ninety with some terrible disease! Of course Frankie can have her friends round. I don't want to put our normal life on hold for the next seven months."

Good old Mum. Dad looked at her over the

top of his glasses and shrugged his shoulders in a resigned sort of way.

"Just try and be a bit considerate, won't you?" he said, before going back to reading his paper.

I told the others the next day that we could have the sleepover at my place on Saturday. I also warned them that we wouldn't be able to get up to the same sort of noisy stunts as usual, because of Mum.

"I remember my mum being really ill when she was expecting Callum," Fliss told us. "She was sick all the time, it was awful!"

"Mum's fine," I told them. "It's Dad I'm worried about."

"Don't worry, Frankie," said Rosie soothingly. "We'll be too busy working on our competition entry to get into any trouble."

Hmm. I wasn't so sure that I believed that. But I worked really hard to get ready for the sleepover so that Mum wouldn't have to do anything. I tidied my room and I cleaned up in the kitchen. I even offered to prepare the supper for everyone on Saturday evening, but

Dad said that was OK, he'd make one of his famous scrummy pizzas.

We've had tons of sleepovers now, so I know this sounds crazy, but I was really nervous about this one. It's hard to explain, but I guess I was worried that the others would think it was boring if we didn't do our usual wacky stuff like International Gladiators. I felt sort of caught in the middle: Dad wanted us to be quiet and I was sure that my friends would expect us to be as loud as normal. Somehow I had to keep everyone happy.

By the time five o'clock on Saturday came, I'd got myself in a right old state. I was still tidying up everywhere as I waited for the first person to arrive.

"Honestly, Frankie. If you get any more wound up, you'll snap!" laughed Mum. "Chill out! Isn't that what you say? What's the matter with you anyway?"

"I just don't want you to get all frazzled because my friends are here," I explained.

"Frankie, I love your friends coming round

46

and I am not an invalid," Mum said firmly. "Now will you please just enjoy yourself. It's like living with my mother, for goodness sake!"

We both laughed, and I felt much better.

Suddenly there was a knock at the door. It was Fliss.

"Hiya Frankie, hello Mrs Thomas," she said, thrusting a bag towards us. "Mum says that ginger's very good for morning sickness and she sent you this." Mum took a bottle of murky-coloured liquid out of the bag and looked kind of puzzled.

"Well Fliss, I'll certainly bear that in mind," she smiled. "I must call your mum to thank her."

When she had gone into the lounge, Fliss whispered loudly, "You know, Mum says that she thinks your mum is very brave having another baby at her age. She said she wouldn't want to start with all that again!"

I just hoped that Mum hadn't heard that. Fortunately there was another knock at the door. When I answered it, Kenny, Lyndz and Rosie all bundled in.

"I didn't know that you were all coming together," moaned Fliss. "Why didn't anyone tell me?"

"Don't get your knickers in a twist!" warned Kenny. "Lyndz's dad passed Rosie and me on the way here and gave us a lift. OK?"

Oh-oh, trouble already. That was the last thing I needed.

"Coke anyone?" I asked quickly. "Then we can hit the keyboard, surf the Net and get ready to win this competition."

Everyone dumped their stuff in the hall and we dived into the kitchen. Kenny was doing her usual trick with the Jaffa cakes when Dad walked in.

'Oh no, Dad's going to hit the roof!' I thought.

"Really Kenny, what *are* you doing?" he boomed in his loud lawyer's voice.

Even Kenny, who's as tough as anything, went red and looked dead nervous.

"Look, you should do this with them," Dad said, taking a whole pile of Jaffa cakes. He squashed them down until they were a crumby mush then shoved them into *his* mouth. It was too, *too* gross!

"Hey, cool Mr T!" gasped Kenny.

"Just remember, I'm grown-up and I've got a bigger mouth than you, so don't overdo it, will you?" laughed Dad as he walked back out into the garden.

Maybe I had nothing to worry about after all.

We took our drinks upstairs, and then the others went back down for their sleepover kits. Kenny always shares my bed when we have a sleepover here, just because I'm used to the way she flings herself around in her sleeping bag. This time it was Lyndz's and Rosie's turn to go on the bunk beds, and Fliss was on the camp-bed. Of course, she moaned about that, but it was her turn and 'fair's fair' as my gran always says.

When everyone had finally got their stuff sorted on the right bed, and Fliss had taken half an hour arranging her pyjamas just so, we were ready to go on the Internet. Mum came up and keyed in the password.

"I hope you've got some good ideas for this Home Page competition," she said. "I bet there'll be loads of entries for it."

It was the first time that we'd really thought about it. I mean, the Leicester Mercury covers a wide area. There were bound to be thousands of other kids who were determined to win the first prize too.

"Don't worry about us Mrs T," said Kenny. "We'll come up with a wicked design!"

"I'm sure you will Kenny," laughed Mum, and left us to it.

"I thought we could see if anyone else has a Home Page for a Sleepover Club," I explained, typing in the 'search' box. There were no matches found which was good in one way because it meant that no other Sleepover Club had a web site so at least our idea was original. But, then again we were really looking for ideas for our Home Page design.

"Well, can't we go into another web site?" asked Rosie. "What about looking up Brownies?"

"Hey, that's a good idea!" I nodded. I can

always rely on Rosie for a sensible suggestion, which is more than I can say for the others.

I typed 'Brownies' in the 'search' box, and there were hundreds of matches this time. It was really cool going into some of the web sites and reading about different Brownie packs all round the country. Some of the stuff they'd been doing sounded really wild.

"We should set up one of these for our pack," suggested Kenny. "Maybe we could get a computer badge out of it too."

"Yeah, that's a good idea," agreed Lyndz. "I've still got a few spaces on my sash to fill up."

"Do you think we should be making notes?" asked Fliss quietly. "Just so we remember what kind of thing we should include on the design?"

"Good thinking, Batman!" I agreed. "Pens to the ready!"

Everyone dived into their bags for notebooks and pens and we started scribbling down ideas.

After a while there was a knock on my door.

"Erm, sorry, I must have the wrong room," my Dad said, looking at us in amazement. "My daughter wouldn't be *working* on a Saturday. Maybe you're alien clones of her and her friends. You certainly look genuine enough!"

He picked up my hand and started to sniff it.

"Ooh Dad, don't be gross!" I laughed.

"I came to tell you that pizza's ready!" he said. "Did you know that you've been on the Internet over an hour? Surely you've got enough stuff by now!"

We all nodded, but I couldn't believe we'd been there so long.

The pizza was fab, as usual. But we kind of gobbled it down because we were all really keen to get back to my room and start working on our competition design. As I left the table, Dad whispered,

"Thanks for being so quiet, Frankie. We really appreciate it!"

Actually I hadn't had to say anything to the others. We were just so involved in our ideas that we didn't want to act crazy. Famous last words or what?

We were all trying to come up with ideas for the Home Page, when Fliss suddenly piped up, "Who's going to get the computer if we win it anyway?"

I hadn't actually given that much thought. "We'll have to share it I guess," I replied.

"But you don't need it because you've already got one," Fliss pointed out. "And so has Rosie."

"Well, the rest of you will have to share it then, won't you?"

"But wouldn't it be better if it was in one place?" Fliss asked. "I mean you can't keep dismantling it every five minutes, can you? It'd never work then."

"Oh I get it," snarled Kenny. "You think *you* should have it, don't you Fliss?"

"N...not really," stammered Fliss. "Maybe we should have a competition ourselves. Whoever comes up with the best design for the Home Page gets to keep the computer!"

We all looked at her as though she'd gone crazy.

"I don't think that's fair!" Rosie piped up.

Kenny, Lyndz and I burst out laughing because it's usually Fliss who goes on about things not being fair.

"Look, let's not fall out about this now," I said. "We've got to win the competition to start with. Let's cross that other bridge when we come to it!"

"As your gran always says," the others chimed in.

You can sense that there was a bit of bad feeling creeping in, can't you? Well, let me tell you, it got much worse.

CHAPTER FIVE

To be honest with you, at first I thought that everything was back to normal between us all. We settled down to sorting out our Home Page design and everything was cool. Lyndz suggested that we should have a photograph of the Sleepover Club all together at the top of the page.

"You mean so that anyone surfing the Net might stumble across it and think. 'Wow! Who are those gorgeous creatures?'" Kenny said, putting on a silly voice.

"They'll think it's a horror show and surf on to something else, more like!" laughed Lyndz.

"We could have individual photos as well,"

suggested Rosie, "and write a few lines about what we like and don't like."

Everybody was nodding and agreeing. So it was a complete shock when everything suddenly went pear-shaped.

I blame Fliss really. I know that we tend to blame Fliss for most things, but she never really knows when to keep quiet. I mean, when everybody was happy, was it really the right time to bang on again about who was going to look after the computer? No, of course it wasn't. I don't worry about things until I have to. And I certainly didn't see any point in worrying about a computer we hadn't even won yet. Fliss is different: she *always* has to have something to worry about.

"I just think we ought to sort it out now!" she kept saying.

"But what's the point?" I asked her. "We haven't won it yet!"

"I just like to know these things!" Fliss replied.

"Why do you always have to make everything so complicated?" asked Rosie crossly. "If anyone should look after the computer, it should be me. My house has the most room and we could use my bedroom as the Sleepover Club Headquarters."

Now we all turned to stare at Rosie.

"You've got a computer already!" I told her. "Besides, the Sleepover Club's not that kind of club."

"Well maybe it should be, we've got membership cards and everything, haven't we?" she said. "We should make it official, and my room would be the best place to hold our meetings in."

It was the first time Rosie had been so firm about something. She usually just goes with the flow. Now it looked as though she had her own ideas and wanted to change everything about the Sleepover Club.

"Look here, Rosie-Posie," said Kenny menacingly. "You haven't been a member of the Club as long as the rest of us, so don't try to change how we do things. We can always withdraw your membership, you know!"

I couldn't quite believe that she'd said that.

Kenny sometimes opens her mouth before she's put her brain into action. But I guess she was just mad about someone wanting to change the Sleepover Club.

Lyndz could see that things were getting a bit hairy, with Rosie and Kenny glaring at each other, so she did her usual peace-making bit.

"Look guys, the whole point of the Sleepover Club is to have fun, isn't it?" she asked. "You remember fun, don't you?"

"You mean this?" asked Kenny and wrestled Rosie on to the ground. A big bottle of Coke for our midnight feast was in the way and it crashed to the floor. Fortunately it didn't burst – that would have been a disaster.

I wasn't sure whether the wrestling was fun or serious to be honest, so I was really relieved when Mum knocked on the door and came in.

"Hey girls!" she said, looking at Kenny and Rosie writhing on the ground. "Is everything all right?"

"Yes, of course!" I said, almost too brightly. Kenny and Rosie stopped their wrestling and, rather flushed, stood up.

"Well I just came in to say goodnight," Mum continued. "I'm kind of tired and I'm going to bed. It might be a good idea if you went too. It's after ten."

"OK Mum," I said. "We're ready for bed anyway."

"Good, and if you could keep the noise down I'd appreciate it," Mum smiled. "I need enough beauty sleep for two now!"

When she'd gone, Kenny and Rosie were still glaring at each other.

"Please can you two just make up?" I pleaded. "Let's get ready and have our midnight feast. We're always happier with chocolate inside us!"

We were all kind of subdued getting ready for bed, which was not like us at all. I felt desperate to make everything all right again.

"Look, food!" I said, tipping everybody's goodies all over my bed. "Come and get it!"

"I'm thirsty!" said Rosie, grabbing the bottle of Coke from the floor. She opened it – and I'm not kidding, it fizzed up and flew *everywhere*.

It went all over Kenny's sleeping bag, all over the sweets spread over the bed and all over the computer. But worse than that, it went all over Kenny.

I don't know how the next bit happened, but somehow, as soon as she was caught in this shower of Coke, Kenny ducked and sort of lost her balance. She seemed to be staggering about for ages, but it can't really have been more than a few seconds. Unfortunately though, she staggered right into the computer table and ended up knocking the keyboard on to the floor with a huge crash.

Whilst all that was happening the rest of us were either laughing or screaming. Whatever we were doing, we were doing it pretty loudly, because before we knew it Mum and Dad had come haring into my room and were surveying the scene of destruction.

"What on earth…!" shouted Dad. "What's happened to the computer?"

He picked up the keyboard from the floor and examined it. Then he wiped the sticky mess off the computer screen.

"Luckily for you the computer was turned off!" he said crossly. "I'd hate to think what might have happened if it had still been on. I'll have to check the keyboard properly in the morning."

He looked tired and angry at the same time.

"I might have known that you couldn't stay quiet for too long!" he said with a sigh. "I'm disappointed in you, Frankie, I thought you were more mature than that."

Lyndz started to explain that it wasn't my fault, but he just held up his hand.

"Save it Lyndsey," he said. "I'm too tired for all this now."

He went out. Mum just looked at me and shrugged her shoulders. Then she left too.

I felt awful. I really felt as though I had let them down.

"I'm really sorry Frankie," said Rosie, rushing over to me. "That was all my fault."

"It was mine too," admitted Kenny. "We'll explain everything in the morning, won't we?"

Rosie nodded.

Lyndz could see that I looked upset. "Don't worry Frankie, it'll be OK. Everyone's just tired, that's all. I know that I am." She gave a massive yawn. "I just need a few fizzy fish to help me to sleep!"

We all giggled and made a grab for the rather sticky sweets that were scattered over Kenny's sleeping bag. By the time we'd been munching in to our feast for five minutes or so, we were all laughing and joking. It was as though all the friction between Kenny and Rosie had never happened. I was glad about that. I just hoped that in the morning all the tension between Dad and me would have gone too.

To be honest with you I didn't sleep very well. I felt so bad that I'd let Mum and Dad down. I was awake really early and crept downstairs to make them some tea.

"I'm really, really sorry about what happened," I told them when I took it into their bedroom. "It won't happen again."

"I hope not," said Dad, but he didn't sound

angry like he had done the night before.

When I got back to my room the others were all awake and up, which was a miracle. Even Kenny was sorting out all her stuff and Kenny is *not* a morning person!

"What are you up to?" I asked them suspiciously.

"We thought we'd get up and help you make breakfast, then your Dad might not be so cross with us," explained Lyndz.

They're pretty great, my friends. But looking at their faces, I couldn't help thinking that there was another reason for this sudden burst of generosity. I puzzled over it all the time we were making breakfast.

As Rosie was making the toast she said, "Do you think your parents will ever let us come round again? To sleep over, I mean?"

"I should think so," I said. "In 2010!"

"Not next week then?" asked Kenny, as she set the table.

"You must be joking!" I laughed. "If the computer's damaged, he'll never want to see you lot again. Neither will I, come to that."

The others were looking at each other again, and I was beginning to feel left out.

"Stop doing that!" I shouted. "What is your problem?"

"Well the thing is…" began Lyndz.

"…we didn't design our Home Page last night and the deadline for the competition is a week on Monday," spluttered Fliss.

"…and with homework and netball practice and stuff, we won't have time to do it in the week," continued Rosie.

"So we really need another sleepover… next Friday," concluded Kenny.

"Can't we have it at one of your houses?" I asked.

"We really need the Internet for reference," explained Lyndz. "You know, to make sure we put the right sort of stuff on our Home Page."

That certainly made sense. But then I remembered how cross Dad had been the night before. And to make matters worse, I could hear him and Mum coming downstairs.

"Look," I told the others, "you'll have to leave it with me. Don't mention it now, for goodness sake. I'll have to pick my moment."

I'm sure that Mum and Dad must have known that we had something up our sleeves, but they didn't say anything. Rosie and Kenny apologised about the night before and everyone seemed happy enough.

When the others went home I told them, "I'll work on Mum and Dad about the sleepover, don't worry!"

But to be honest with you, *I* was worried. Getting Dad to let my crazy friends have another sleepover so soon was going to take absolutely all my powers of persuasion.

CHAPTER SIX

Mum and Dad didn't know what had hit them over the next few days. When I wasn't apologising I was washing up, making cups of tea or running errands. But I just couldn't find the right moment to ask them about having another sleepover. Every time I thought about it, I got butterflies in my tummy, my tongue got stuck to the roof of my mouth and I just couldn't do it.

By Wednesday my friends were getting a bit annoyed.

"You're going to have to ask them tonight," said Rosie, "because we've got to get the Home Page finished for the competition."

"When's the deadline?" I asked.

"Monday at 5pm," Rosie replied. "So if we finish it on Friday night, we can post it on Saturday and it should get there in time."

"But we haven't even decided what to put on our Home Page!" I said, feeling really flustered.

"Look Frankie, anybody would think you didn't want us to win or something," said Kenny. She sounded quite cross. "We're going to use a photograph of us all together at the top of the page and we each need to find an individual photo that we like. Then we've got to write a few lines about our likes and dislikes…"

"…and mention a few of our favourite sleepovers," explained Fliss patiently.

It certainly sounded as though the others knew what we had to do, even if I didn't.

"So all *you* have to do Frankie…" said Lyndz meaningfully.

"…is persuade Mum and Dad to let us have the sleepover at my place, yes I know!" I sighed.

I knew that I would have to ask Mum and Dad that evening – and I was dreading it. I got myself in such a state that I couldn't even eat my supper.

"What on earth's the matter, Frankie?" asked Mum. "You'll wear a hole in that plate if you push your food round on it much more."

"It's just… er… about the sleepover," I stammered.

"I think we can forget about that now, Frankie," Mum said calmly.

"Well no, the thing is, we need to have another one to finish our entry for the competition and we should have it here because we'll need to check other web sites on the Internet," I explained, but it all came out in a rush.

Dad put down his fork and looked at me.

"You seriously expect us to have your friends here again after last week's shenanigans?" he asked.

"Yes, no, I don't know," I spluttered.

"Well I don't know either, Frankie. We can't risk all that chaos again," Dad went on. "You almost broke the computer last time, if you remember. Fortunately for you, the keyboard wasn't damaged in the fall."

I looked down at my plate.

"Just wait a minute, Gwyn," Mum said. "What happened wasn't even Frankie's fault. Kenny and Rosie told us that they were responsible. Besides, we've had worse sleepovers. I thought Fliss had killed Kenny at one, don't you remember?"

We all started to laugh, thinking about that little performance.

"Frankie might not be able to have her friends here so much next year, with the baby and everything," Mum continued, "so I think we should let her enjoy her sleepovers while she can."

Dad shrugged his shoulders. Then he smiled, and I knew that he was going to give in. I rushed round and gave them both a big hug.

"You will keep those friends of yours under control though, won't you, Frankie?" asked Dad.

"Sure will!" I shouted back as I rushed to the phone to give the others the good news.

Of course, then I only had a day to get everything ready for our sleepover. Choosing the photos for the Home Page was the hardest part. I found loads with us all together but I couldn't find a good one of me by myself. I don't know about you, but I always look a complete geek in photos. I aim to look all sophisticated and end up looking like Bart Simpson. But if I thought mine was bad, you ought to see have seen the ones the others had chosen. They made the Addams family look like the Spice Girls.

In fact, checking out each other's photos was the first thing we did when everyone had arrived for the sleepover on Friday. We sat in the middle of my bedroom floor with the photos spread around us. Kenny had chosen a photograph of herself in her Leicester City strip – what else? – and Lyndz's showed her in her riding gear. Rosie was looking funky in her jeans and baseball cap and Fliss, well Fliss was posing like some supermodel in what looked like a net curtain. We didn't say anything though, because I don't think any of us could face one of Fliss's moods. My photo just showed me grinning and gawky with my great long legs looking silly in my shorts. The others all thought it looked good though.

We'd found lots of photographs of us all together. But on all of them, at least one of us seemed to be pulling a funny face. And the trouble with photographs is that they bring back so many memories too. So we couldn't just look at them and pick out the one we wanted to use, we had to talk about where they were taken and what we had done – you know how it is. We eventually picked one out with us all in our Brownie uniforms. But when Mum called us for supper we hadn't done *anything* about the Home Page design.

"Look guys," I told the others when we were back upstairs after we'd eaten, "we're going to have to get a move on with this. We've got to post it tomorrow, remember, and right now all we've got are a few photographs."

"Why don't we go on the Internet and have a look at some Home Pages?" suggested Rosie. "It'll probably give us some inspiration."

"Very good thinking, Batman," I said approvingly.

I was just going to call down for Mum when Fliss said, "It's OK, I know what the password is."

I couldn't believe it when she sat down at the computer, typed something in and 'Hey Presto' the Internet came on.

"You little sneak!" shouted Kenny.

"I can't believe you actually *peeped* when we were here before," Rosie turned on her accusingly.

"Look never mind about that now," I said. "We'd better be quick before Mum and Dad catch us!"

Some of the Home Pages were really cool with moving logos and video clips. Lyndz was desperate for us to have something like that in ours but I had to remind her that we were running out of time and we'd have to make do with our photographs.

Kenny suddenly said, "Frankie, I think your mum is coming! She'll go mad if she sees us on the Internet! We aren't supposed to know the password!"

Panic or what! I fiddled about with the mouse, trying to log off as we heard the clomp-clomp-clomp up the stairs. I only just made it!

"Is everything all right, girls?" Mum asked, poking her head round the door just as the computer screen went blank. "I thought you wanted to go on the Internet."

"M...maybe later," I stammered. "We'd better get on and start typing everything up if we want to get the competition entry finished in time."

"OK, just give me a shout when you need me," Mum said, and went out again.

"Phew, that was close!" I sighed. "Mum and Dad would never trust me again if they thought I'd been logging on without them. Just don't tell me the password, Fliss, because I don't want to know."

Fliss looked suitably shame-faced and

shook her head.

"Right let's get started on our entry," I said.
I typed:

WELCOME TO THE SLEEPOVER CLUB

"I'll leave spaces where we're going to put our
photos," I explained. "Like this."

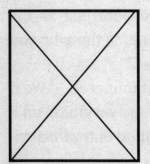 Hi my name's
Francesca Thomas
but my friends call
me Frankie. I like
chocolate, kittens
and the colour
silver. I dislike
spiders, cold mornings and maths
homework. I LOVE sleepovers.

"Right who's going to go next?" I asked.

Fliss began to type about herself while the
rest of us decided what should go on the rest
of the Home Page.

"We need to let people know what the

Sleepover Club is all about," I said. "We could describe our sleepover kit and say what kind of stuff we like to eat at our midnight feasts."

"I've got a photo of us eating it too!" laughed Lyndz. "Look!"

We all giggled when we saw the photo of us with our mouths full of marshmallows. Then we began to write. I couldn't believe how well we worked as a team. Whilst one person was typing things up on the computer, the rest of us were either doing illustrations or planning how everything should look on the finished design.

"It's a pity we haven't got a video of our International Gladiator games to put on the Home Page!" Kenny laughed. Rosie jumped on her back and they leapt around the room pretending to be on a show-jumping course. They galloped over the camp-bed, leapt over me and Fliss who were huddled together on the floor, and started to bounce on top of my bed. Of course, Mum and Dad just had to pick that moment to come into my room, didn't they?

You should have seen the look on Dad's face. I'm sure he thought they were fighting again. But he soon realised that they were just playing.

"How's it going?" Mum asked. "Is the winning entry finished yet?"

"Nearly," I replied. "We've just got to print everything out, glue in the photographs and illustrations and we're done!"

"Well it looks as though we've got a few budding techno-journalists here," laughed Mum.

"Just remember where it all began when you're driving round in your Porsches with buckets of money!" quipped Dad. "And remember that even computer whizz-kids need their beauty sleep. So when you've finished that it's bed, OK?"

"Sure thing Dad," I promised.

When Mum and Dad had gone, Lyndz started yawning. "I am getting kind of tired," she admitted.

"And kind of hungry," said Kenny, rubbing her tummy.

"OK, let's just stick on the photos and drawings, and then we can have our midnight feast," I told them. I printed everything out and turned off the computer. Then we settled down to work, being careful not to crease the paper or make it too sticky with glue. When it was finished we stood back and admired our handiwork. It looked really great.

"I'm sure we're going to win, you know," said Rosie confidently. "I can't believe anyone's entry will be better than ours."

I didn't want to think about that. I just wanted to get ready for bed and tuck into the food.

I moved our Home Page design on to the desk.

"Last one to the bathroom's a pile of poo!" I yelled, shooting out of the door. The others scrambled after me and we all squashed ourselves through the door of the bathroom. It was kind of wild, washing and brushing our teeth like sardines. But of course we had other things on our mind – like food! As soon as we got back to my room, we delved into our sleepover bags.

"Chocs away!" yelled Kenny and poured her bag of midnight feast goodies on to my bed. Everyone else did the same and soon we were tucking into Chupa-Chup lollies, fun-size Mars bars and Milky Way stars.

"Does anyone fancy a drink?" asked Rosie, taking a giant bottle of Coke from her bag.

"Just be careful," I warned. "Remember what happened last time!"

We each held out a plastic beaker and Rosie poured us all a drink.

"My fingers are covered in chocolate," laughed Kenny. "I can hardly hold the cup. I'd better w…w…whheee!"

Before she could put down her cup it slipped out of her hands – all over the desk and all over our perfect Home Page competition entry. She tried to grab the papers out of the Coke, but her hands were too chocolatey. The rest of us could only watch in disbelief as all our hard work turned into a brown slimy mess.

CHAPTER SEVEN

"You've ruined our work!" I screamed when I found my voice. "I can't believe you could have been so clumsy!"

"It's taken us hours to finish that competition entry," moaned Fliss. "We'll never be able to do it all again."

"Even the photos are ruined," said Rosie sadly, taking the dripping pieces of paper from Kenny.

"Hic!" said Lyndz. She always gets hiccups when there's any excitement.

"I'm sorry," said Kenny in a small voice. "It really was an accident."

I know that Kenny can be a bit of a clown

sometimes, but I knew that even she wouldn't deliberately mess up something we'd worked so hard on.

There was a knock at the door and Dad came in.

"What's all the noise?" he asked wearily. "I thought you were going to bed."

"We are," I said quickly. "We've just had our midnight feast. We'll be going to bed in a minute, promise!."

Dad looked at me as though he didn't quite believe me. But I didn't want him to find out that we'd ruined our Home Page entry. I thought he'd never trust us to have another sleepover ever again. The others all crowded round the desk so that he couldn't see all the Coke in a pool on top of it. Lyndz was still hiccupping, but she was trying to swallow them and somehow they sounded louder than ever.

"Try holding your breath Lyndsey," Dad advised. "That's supposed to work. Right you lot, I want to see you in those sleeping bags – now!"

We scrambled into our beds and Dad turned out the light.

"Sleep well," he said. "And don't even think about getting up again, because I'll be listening." With that he closed the door and went back to bed.

We counted to twenty-five, then flicked on the torches which we keep in our sleeping bags.

"Phew, that was close," I said. At least Dad hadn't clocked all the mess on the desk. I leapt out of bed and went to mop it up with a pile of tissues. Then I turned to the others.

"Right," I whispered. "Who wants to win that competition?"

"Me!" they all shouted until I hissed at them to keep quiet. We hardly dared to breathe in case Dad had heard and was going to come storming in. Fortunately for us, he didn't.

"OK, all I've got to do is print out our entry again," I whispered. "We'll have to find more photos and do the drawings again, but that shouldn't take too long."

I turned on the computer and the room was

filled with an eerie green glow. I went through all my files, but I couldn't find our Home Page entry *anywhere*. Then I was hit with an awful heavy feeling.

"I can't find it," I said in a small voice.

"What do you mean, you can't find it?" said Fliss in surprise.

"I was in such a rush when I switched off the computer, I didn't actually save it," I muttered.

There was a horrible silence.

"I don't believe it!" said Kenny in disgust. "You should save everything!"

"Look, Brain-Box, if you hadn't spilt Coke all over our work, we wouldn't be in this mess," I hissed.

"All right you two, we haven't got time to fall out," said Lyndz quickly. "We'll just have to type it out again. Hey guys, did you hear that? No hiccups. They've gone. Maybe I should hold my breath more often!"

"Maybe Kenny should too," I growled.

Fliss meanwhile had started to sob.

"I'm so tired," she moaned. "I can't believe

we've got to do it all again."

"I know," I said gently. "We're all tired, but at least this time we'll know what we're doing. Look, I'll type up my stuff on the computer first, then we'll do everything in the same order as last time. Can everybody remember what they wrote?"

The others all nodded.

"OK, let's get to it!" I said.

It was kind of weird working so late at night, especially as we could only work by torchlight. We daren't put on the main light in case Mum or Dad noticed it. We did have a scare though when we heard Mum moving about. We all scrambled back into bed and held our breath. I'd left the computer on, and for an awful moment I thought that she might see the light under the door and come in. If she'd turned off the computer then we'd have been right back to square one. Fortunately she didn't seem to notice it. So when we were sure that she had gone back to bed, we all got up again and carried on.

"I am so tired," mumbled Lyndz, slumping

over the computer keyboard. "All my words are coming out wrong."

I looked at the screen, and saw that she'd written:

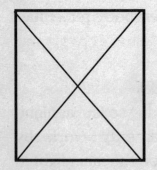

Mt namd iz Lymsey,
bette knowm az
Lynsx tp Mi frins.
I lov horse ridig,
eetin and playimn
netbal I don't
lik mi tow younge
broters. My favorit part Of our slepoves iz the midnigt fest.

"Hmm, I see what you mean!" I gave a small laugh which turned into a huge yawn. "I don't think you'd better type any more, Lyndz. We've nearly finished anyway. If you go and sort out the photographs I'll finish off here."

I think it was about 1.30am when we were finally sticking all our drawings and photographs on to our new Home Page competition entry. We'd had to use Fliss's photograph from the old soggy entry because she hadn't brought a spare one. It was a bit sticky and Fliss of course moaned about it, but to be honest with you, we were past caring. We only had one competition entry form too and that had got a bit Coke-stained, so we had to dry it off over the radiator. It got a bit crinkled up, but as Rosie said, it didn't matter what it looked like as long as we had one.

On the form there was space for just one name and address. And, as you know, that's the kind of thing which usually sparks off huge arguments amongst the Sleepover Club. Not this time. We were just too tired for that.

"You put your name down Frankie," suggested Kenny. "We've done all the work here so we might as well use this address."

The others agreed. So I wrote everything down as neatly as I could, and breathed a sigh of relief that we'd finally finished.

I can't tell you how great it felt to flop into bed. We were totally exhausted. Mum couldn't believe it when she actually had to wake us up the next morning.

"Anybody'd think you'd been up all night!" she laughed. "You're not usually as tired as this, even when you've been playing those wild games of yours. It must be old age creeping up on you!"

"Ha, ha!" I said, snuggling further down into my sleeping bag.

"Breakfast'll be ready in ten minutes," she called as she went out. "*If* you can manage to get up for it!"

"I guess we ought to get up!" I yawned.

"You bet!" shouted Lyndz, suddenly coming to life. "I'm really hungry after working all night."

"Mmm, so am I, now you come to mention it," laughed Rosie.

The only person who had real problems getting up was Kenny – as usual. She looked as though she could have stayed in bed all day. Unfortunately for her, she had her badminton class to go to.

We finally made it downstairs and were munching into our toast when Dad asked us if he could have a look at our Home Page entry before we posted it.

"Hmm, very impressive," he said when he'd read it. "But why is the form all brown and crinkled?"

My heart was thumping, but I tried to look as cool as possible. "It got... a bit wet!" I spluttered.

"I won't ask," Dad said, looking at us all strangely, "because I'm not sure that I want to know!"

"Do you think we should present our entry in a folder or something?" asked Rosie after a while. "To make it stand out a bit?"

"They do always say that judges notice things which are presented a bit differently," Mum said.

"I know!" shrieked Fliss, suddenly leaping up.

"Are you all right, Felicity?" asked Dad. "You've gone a very funny colour."

Fliss was bright red with excitement. "I was just thinking," she stammered. "Mum has leaflets for her beauty therapy bound in plastic covers at a place up the High Street.

They look dead posh. I'm going shopping with her this morning and I could take our Home Page there. It would look ever so good and the judges would be bound to notice it."

The rest of us looked at each other. It wasn't that we didn't trust Fliss. We'd all seen her mum's leaflets enough times, and they did look classy. It's just that Fliss can be, well, a bit dippy.

"But we've got to post it today," I reminded her. "Will you have enough time? Shouldn't we just post it now?"

"I'll have bags of time," Fliss promised. "I'll even go to the Post Office and put the right stamps on too."

"But we should *all* be there to post it," said Rosie. "It is a joint effort after all."

"What time's the last post on a Saturday?" I asked Mum.

"12.30 at the box on the corner," she replied.

"OK, can we all meet there at quarter past twelve then?" I asked.

The others all said that they could. Kenny

would have finished her badminton by then, Rosie was going home to help do the shopping but could get back in time, and Lyndz was staying with me for the morning until her dad could pick her up to take her riding in the afternoon. Fliss was of course going out with her mum.

Dad gave us an envelope to put our entry in, and Rosie addressed it because she's got the neatest handwriting. Then we all coughed up some money to Fliss for the cover and the postage.

"You will be back in time, won't you Fliss?" I asked her for the hundredth time when her mum called for her.

"Yes," she sighed impatiently. "How many more times? You should be grateful to me that I'm getting this done for you!"

The rest of us rolled our eyes.

"What is she like?" said Kenny.

When the others had gone and Lyndz and I were left by ourselves, I admitted that I had a funny feeling about letting Fliss loose with something so important.

"A sort of a 'something's-going-to-go-wrong' feeling?" Lyndz asked.

"Mmm," I nodded.

"Me too!" said Lyndz grimly.

CHAPTER EIGHT

Whilst Lyndz was with me we had a really cool time playing around on the Internet. I finally had the chance to look up 'horses' for her, seeing as she's so nuts about them. There were millions of web sites so Lyndz was well pleased.

After a while though, she said, "Actually Frankie, there's a favour I've been meaning to ask you."

"Oh yes?" I wondered what on earth it could be.

She took a scrumpled piece of paper from her bag.

"My grandparents in Holland are on the

Internet and they've sent me their email address. Do you think I could send them a message using your computer?"

Now, I'd been a bit confused about all this email lark myself. Dad had explained that it's just a way of sending computer messages to other people. It's brilliant because they get them almost immediately, no matter where they are in the world. Sending a message to Lyndz's grandparents would be a fab chance to see how it all worked. I called Dad and asked him to show us how it was done.

"It's really easy," he told us. "You just go into the Mail facility, put the email address of the person you're sending the message to, and briefly say what it's about. Then all you have to do is type your message and post it by clicking the mouse on the 'post' box."

It all seemed pretty easy, so Lyndz typed:

```
Hi there Gran and Grandad. I
hope you're well. I'm typing
this on Frankie's computer
because she's just got signed on
```

to the Internet. Please send me a
message soon.
Love Lyndsey XXX

"How will they know where to send a reply
to?" I asked Dad.

"It will show our email address on their
computer when they pick up their message,"
Dad explained. "Our computer will be like a
postal service for messages between Lyndsey
and her grandparents."

"Speaking about postal services," I said, "I
hope Fliss manages to get everything done in
time to post our entry off."

"I'm sure she will," said Dad as he left the
room. "It sounded simple enough to have a
cover put on your work."

Lyndz and I looked at each other. Where
Fliss is concerned, nothing is ever simple.

Before we knew it, it was almost twelve. Lyndz
and I ran out to the postbox where Kenny was
already waiting. Rosie's mum dropped her off
just after we'd got there.

"I can't wait to see our entry!" she squeaked. "I bet it looks fantastic now. We're bound to win with it, don't you think?"

"As long as Fliss hasn't had it covered in lime green or something," said Kenny.

"Here she is now!" beamed Lyndz. "Let's ask her!"

Fliss was walking slowly towards us.

"Let's see it!" we all yelled, running up the road to meet her.

"Where is it, then?" asked Kenny. "Is it in your bag? Come on, give us a look!" And she started to prod about in Fliss's shoulder bag.

"Don't do that!" Fliss snapped. She was all white and looked kind of funny.

"Are you all right, Fliss?" I asked, suddenly worried.

Fliss's chin wobbled. "I just don't want everyone pushing around me," she said.

We all stood back so that we weren't crowding her.

"I bet you've been rushing, haven't you?" asked Rosie sympathetically.

Fliss nodded.

"Yes, well, we're sorry that you're tired and that, but where's the entry?" asked Kenny. "We want to see it before we post it."

Fliss started rooting about in her bag, then stopped.

"I've, er…" she stammered.

"It must be in there somewhere," snapped Kenny, grabbing her bag from her.

"It's not," blurted Fliss tragically. "I've lost it!"

"You've done WHAT?" I yelled.

"Imusthaveputtheenvelopedownsome whereandIcan'tfindit," she gabbled very fast. "When I got home, I didn't have it with me."

The others all started yelling, but I tried to stay as calm as possible.

"Well, where did you have it last? Did you go to the shop to get the cover put on it?"

"Of course I did," Fliss snapped. "I'm not completely stupid, you know."

Kenny muttered something under her breath.

"Look, time is running out," I said quickly. "Could you have left it in another shop?"

"I must have done. I went to the Post Office and bought the stamps, but I didn't seal up the envelope because I wanted you all to see how great it looked before we posted it."

I looked at my watch. It was already after twelve, and we didn't have much time.

"We're going to have to go back and look for it," I told the others. I could see Dad in the garden, so I shouted to him to see if he could give us a lift to the shops. He said that he would, and we all piled into our estate car.

It only took a few minutes to drive to the High Street but it felt like *forever*. Dad dropped us outside the Post Office, and I told him that we'd walk home.

"Where did you go from here?" I asked Fliss.

"Well, I went into that greengrocer's with Mum," began Fliss, pointing over the road. "Then I went into the newsagent's to buy the new *Girl Talk* and I got some sweets as well, pear drops, lovely, do you want one?" She held out the bag.

"No!" I said through gritted teeth. The others took one.

"After that I went to the chemist to look at the new make-up, they've got some lovely pinky-purple lipstick and nail varnish to match…"

"Fliss, will you shut up!" I yelled. "We don't need to know every single detail about your shopping trip. We're trying to find our Home Page, remember? The one you lost?"

Fliss's eyes filled with tears.

"Look, I'm sorry," I said more gently, "but this is kind of important and we are running out of time. We'll have to split up. Kenny, you go into the greengrocer's, Lyndz can go into the newsagent's and I'll go into the chemist. Fliss and Rosie, you see if you can think of anywhere else it could be."

The others nodded and we all ran into the shops.

The chemist was busy with crying babies and their frazzled mothers. It took me ages to find someone I could ask about our envelope. When I did ask the woman behind the counter, she went to see if the owner knew anything about it. She came back and said she was sorry but they hadn't had anything handed in. I just hoped that the others had found it. But when I got outside, everyone was still empty-handed. We'd checked everywhere, but no-one had seen our envelope.

"That's it," I mumbled as we dejectedly walked back home. "All that hard work for nothing."

Suddenly a car horn blasted. I nearly jumped out of my skin, and turned to see Fliss's mum pulling up beside us.

"Frankie's dad told me you'd be here. Look what I've found!" she said, thrusting an envelope towards us. It was our Home Page competition entry!

"Where was it?" gasped Fliss.

"It had got muddled up with some of my shopping," Fliss's mum explained. "I found it when I was unpacking my bags. I told you that might have happened, didn't I Felicity?"

Fliss nodded guiltily.

"You mean you didn't check?" I yelled. "We've trailed round the shops for nothing?"

Fliss looked all red in the face: partly

exhausted and partly embarrassed.

"Well, let's find a postbox and post it – quick!" I shouted.

"But see how great it looks first," insisted Fliss, pulling the entry from the envelope.

Our Home Page did look pretty hot, we had to admit, but there was no time to admire it properly.

"Where's the nearest postbox?" Lyndz asked.

"I'm sure there's one round the corner," said Fliss.

We all started running. Now, this was very familiar. It only seemed like two minutes since we'd been running to catch the post before. Rosie must have remembered that too.

"Hadn't we better double check the address?" she said, coming to a sudden stop. "Remember what happened to that entry for the bedroom makeover competition?"

We all looked at Kenny. We remembered the mix up with addresses only too well.

"Hey, that's not fair!" protested Kenny. "And anyway, I didn't write the envelope this time."

We stopped running and carefully checked the address. Then we started running again. This time, Fliss suddenly ground to a halt.

"Make sure it's sealed properly!" she screamed. "It would be awful if our Home Page design fell out before it even got there."

We all stopped again, and gave the envelope a good lick and press down.

"Stop, start, stop, start," grumbled Kenny. "At this rate…"

"Oh NO!" Rosie wailed, pointing frantically up the road.

We all turned round to look where she was pointing.

"I don't believe it!" I gasped. The others groaned. Fliss gave a little sob.

It was the post van, and it was driving away. We had missed the last post. Now our Home Page competition entry would never get there on time.

CHAPTER NINE

"You are unbelievable, Fliss!" yelled Kenny. "You had one simple thing to do and you messed that up. Any normal person would have checked the shopping first before they got in such a flap. But not you, oh no. Panic first, think later, that's what you always do, isn't it?"

"Well if you hadn't ruined our work the night before, we wouldn't have been up all night. Then I wouldn't have been so tired, would I?" Fliss yelled back. "And if I hadn't been so tired I wouldn't have lost it at all."

"Shush!" I said, trying to calm them both down. I couldn't face any more arguments.

"I can't believe that we worked so hard and our entry isn't even going to get there," sighed Rosie. "I mean, it was *so* good. We would have won first prize for sure. It's like the bedroom makeover competition all over again."

"Well, I don't think we should give in so easily this time," I told them. "At least we've still got our entry, and it hasn't been sent to London by mistake."

Everyone gave Kenny a dirty look. Kenny, for once, was silent.

"We *have* to keep trying," I said.

"But the deadline's on Monday at five o'clock," said Lyndz. "There isn't another post now until Monday morning and that's too late."

Then I was struck by a brainwave. "What's to stop us actually *taking* our entry in?" I asked the others.

We had stopped by my front gate.

"How can we do that?" asked Fliss.

"We need someone to drive us there – tomorrow!" I declared.

While the others were thinking about that,

Mr Collins, Lyndz's dad, drove up in his big van. Kenny, Rosie, Fliss and Lyndz all looked at me with great big grins on their faces. Then we all turned towards him and smiled very, very sweetly.

"Did you have a good sleepover?" he asked. "You certainly look pleased enough with yourselves."

We didn't say anything, we just carried on grinning. Mum and Dad had come to say hello to Mr Collins and they just couldn't work out what was going on either.

"Are you ready for the stables, Lyndsey?" her dad asked, still looking a bit confused. "I've got your riding gear in the van. You can change when you're there."

"Ask him!" I whispered in Lyndz's ear and we pushed her forward.

"Erm, Dad," she began.

"Yes Lyndsey?"

"We were wondering… well, you see, we've got this problem. We missed the post with this competition entry and we need to get it in tomorrow because the deadline's on

Monday. So we need to take it, hic, tomorrow, hic, and, hic…"

"You've got a big van and we could all go together if you'd take us," I continued eagerly.

"And we'd be ever so grateful!" added Rosie.

"And the others will kill me if we don't get the entry in on time," squeaked Fliss, "because it's all my fault!"

Lyndz's dad began to laugh.

"Well if you put it like that Felicity, I don't have much choice, do I? But where exactly am I supposed to be taking you?"

Fliss showed him the address on the envelope. It was the Mercury newspaper office in Leicester.

"Yes, I reckon I can get you there," Lyndz's dad said when he'd looked at it.

We all did high fives and hugged each other.

"Thanks, hic, Dad!" said Lyndz, giving him a big hug.

"You run along and get your stuff, Lyndsey," smiled her father. "And you'd better try to get rid of those hiccups too."

We all ran inside with Lyndz. Whilst Rosie

and Fliss got her sleepover kit together, I worked on trying to get rid of her hiccups. It was no good asking her to hold her breath because she kept giggling.

All of a sudden Kenny let out this really chilling scream.

"What's the matter?" we squealed, nearly jumping out of our skins.

"Nothing," replied Kenny calmly, "but I bet your hiccups have gone, haven't they Lyndz?"

Lyndz gulped a little. "Yes, they have," she nodded. "But you nearly scared me half to death!"

We were still all laughing about that when we went outside.

"Right you lot, it's arranged," said Mr Collins as he took Lyndz's bag from her and put it inside the van. "As it happens I have to go into Leicester tomorrow afternoon anyway. So if the rest of you can get round here to Frankie's by two o'clock, I'll take you to deliver your competition entry."

"Yes!" we all cheered.

"You just make sure you hold on to that

entry form until tomorrow Fliss," I warned her. Fliss just tutted as though she was fed up with the whole thing. But I noticed that her grip on the envelope tightened. I bet she even slept with it that night!

I must admit that for me Sunday couldn't come fast enough. And when it did I watched the clock all morning, but every five minutes seemed like a lifetime. I never thought two o'clock would come. But of course it did. With a bang. Fliss, Rosie and Kenny all arrived together and knocked on the front door so loudly I thought they were a herd of hippos.

"You have got the competition entry, haven't you Fliss?" I asked as soon as I opened the door.

"Of course I have!" she said crossly. "I'm not likely to forget that again, am I?"

Kenny pulled a face behind Fliss's back. Rosie and I spluttered with laughter. But before Fliss could ask what we were laughing about there was a loud hooting outside.

"Right you lot, are you all set?" shouted Mr

Collins from the van as he drew up.

Lyndz was waving at us like a maniac from inside. We all piled in to join her, waved to my mum and dad who had come to the gate with us, and drove off.

Cuddington, where we live, isn't really very far from Leicester, but that Sunday it seemed to take us forever to get there. There seemed to be about a million cars on the road and they were all as slow as tortoises.

"I could run faster than this!" said Kenny through gritted teeth. She started to drum her fingers against the window.

"Will you stop doing that!" yelled Fliss. "You're really getting on my nerves!"

"Then we're just about even," snarled Kenny, "because you're always getting on mine."

"Girls, please!" shouted Mr Collins from the front of the van. "It's bad enough being in this traffic without you two having a go at each other. Let's put some music on. That should cheer things up."

He pushed in a cassette. Some screechy

guitar music blasted out. It was awful. Lyndz's dad quickly turned it off.

"What was that?" I asked.

"One of Stuart's favourite bands!" laughed Lyndz, pulling a face.

"Let's try this one," said her dad, putting on another cassette. This time Boyzone blared out.

"*Cool!*"

We all sang along and we were still singing when Lyndz's dad pulled over and stopped the van.

"Are we here then? Is this it?" asked Fliss excitedly.

"No, I've just got to drop something in here," explained Lyndz's dad. "I'll be two shakes of a cat's tail."

He took a small box from the passenger seat and got out.

"Now stay right here and don't move a muscle!"

We all sort of froze in the position we were in. Then we cracked up laughing.

"I hope we do win the competition," said

Rosie. "That would be so mega. The M&Ms would be as jealous as anything."

"Just imagine a new computer and all those CD-Roms!" said Lyndz.

"And our own Home Page, don't forget that!" laughed Fliss.

"That would be the best thing!" I grinned. "I bet no-one else at school has their own Home Page. People from all over the world will be able to see it. Oh, I almost forgot…" I pulled a crumpled piece of paper out of my pocket. "This came for you last night, Lyndz. I printed it out for you."

Lyndsey unfolded the paper and the others crowded round.

"It's an email message from my grandparents," she explained. "They know some girls our age in Holland who would like some English pen-friends. They've sent us their email addresses so we can get in touch with them."

"Awesome!"

"What's awesome?" asked Lyndz's dad as he climbed into the van.

Lyndsey showed him the message.

"That's great!" he said. "I might have to come round to your place myself, Frankie. At this rate you'll be hearing from my parents more than I do! Right then, let's hit the road for the Leicester Mercury. The address you want isn't far from here."

We set off again. It had got quieter on the road, so it didn't seem two minutes before we could see the Leicester Mercury building in front of us.

"You've gone very quiet, girls," Mr Collins said. "You're not going to tell me that you've forgotten your competition entry, are you?"

Fliss tutted. She always thinks people are criticising her – even when they're joking.

"It just seems a bit strange that after all our hard work we're just going to post our envelope through the door and that's it," I explained. "We should perform a good luck ceremony or something."

The others nodded.

"It feels like we've gone through so much to get our entry here," said Rosie.

"It's only fair that we win the competition now!" said Fliss.

The rest of us cracked up, and Fliss laughed too. "I said that on purpose because you're always teasing me about being fair!" she giggled.

"Nice one Fliss!" we all said, slapping her on the back.

"Right guys, we're here!" said Mr Collins as he stopped the van. "If you're having a good luck ceremony, you'd better be quick because I'm on a double yellow line here. I don't want to get a fine when I'm doing you a good turn, do I?"

"No, that wouldn't be fair at all!" said Fliss, completely straight-faced.

"OK, let's all hold the envelope," I said.

Fliss held it out and we all grabbed hold of it.

"Gently!" I warned the others. "We don't want to spoil it when we've come so far!"

"Now what?" asked Lyndz.

"We'll all close our eyes and concentrate as hard as we can on winning the competition," I said.

After about thirty seconds Fliss whispered, "Can we stop now? It's giving me a headache."

"Yep, I reckon that should do it," said Lyndz's dad. "You'd better go now. There are some security guards in there who are looking at us as though we're mad."

We piled out of the van and over to the office building. Although we looked everywhere for a letter box, we couldn't see one.

"What do we do now?" whispered Fliss.

We were kind of conscious that the security guards inside were watching us.

"We'll just have to go in and ask those men where to take this," said Kenny firmly.

She grabbed the envelope and pushed open the huge glass doors.

"Well, what can we do for you?" asked one of the men. He was very fat and bald and looked a bit frightening at first, but he was very friendly. We explained about our competition entry and how we'd missed the post.

"You just leave it with us!" he said. "We'll make sure that the right person gets it first thing tomorrow morning."

"You won't forget, will you?" said Rosie. "It is very important."

"No, you can trust us!" he promised, and both men laughed. It was more a bellow than a laugh and it sort of echoed round the empty building.

"Thank you!"

We all hurried outside.

"I wouldn't want to be a security guard in an empty building like that," shuddered Rosie. "It would give me the creeps."

"And me," agreed Lyndz. "Let's get out of here."

We ran to where her dad had parked his van, but it wasn't there. Neither was Mr Collins. The street was deserted and he was nowhere to be seen.

CHAPTER TEN

"Where's Dad gone?" asked Lyndz anxiously.

Even I felt a bit panicky inside, but I knew that Mr Collins couldn't have gone far.

"He might have been kidnapped or something!" squeaked Fliss.

"Don't be stupid!" snorted Kenny. "Look, here he is!"

Mr Collins was running towards us.

"I'm sorry about that, girls," he said breathlessly. "A policeman asked me to move on and said there were parking spaces round the corner. They were a bit further away than I'd expected. Anyway, did you deliver your competition entry all right?"

We told him that we'd left it with the security guards.

"Well it'll be in safe hands then, won't it?" he laughed.

We got back to the van, and all the way home we talked about our Home Page. So much had happened since we'd finished it that we couldn't really remember what we'd put. Then we thought of a million things that we *should* have written about. Isn't that always the way – you think of all the good stuff when it's too late!

"When will we hear if we've got first prize?" asked Fliss.

I pulled the newspaper cutting from my pocket. "It says, 'All prize winners will be notified by 5pm on Monday 17th. The judges' decision is final.'" I read out.

"That's two whole weeks!" moaned Fliss. "I don't think I can wait that long!"

"Me neither," agreed Lyndz. "It's too exciting. We'll have to decide what we're going to do with all the prizes when we win them."

I shot her a look. I remembered how we'd

fallen out about the prizes before and I certainly wasn't going to go through that again.

"We'll just have to wait and see whether we win first," I said quickly.

Boy, did the next two weeks drag. But we talked about the Home Page competition every day, so when Monday 17th finally arrived we were really hyped up.

You remember that I'd put my address on the entry form, don't you? Well on Monday morning I flew downstairs as soon as I opened my eyes. I wanted to see whether the post had come. It hadn't.

"You're up early!" said Dad, who was in the kitchen.

I was going to explain why when there was a rattle at the letter box followed by Pepsi's frantic bark. I dashed to the front door. There were three letters on the mat: one boring brown envelope for Dad, a dentist's reminder for all of us, and an advertisement for a new pizza take-away in Cuddington. My heart sank

– there was nothing for me. I felt really numb. Dad came to get the post.

"Hey, what's with the long face?" he asked. "Oh I get it, you haven't heard from the competition, have you?"

I shook my head.

"Well don't look so miserable! There are other ways they can get in touch," he said gently. "I know that they're probably not an expert like you, but I'm sure that someone at the Mercury will be able to use a phone. They've got your number, haven't they?"

"Yes!" I shouted. "They'll probably ring up, won't they? But what if I'm at school? Will Mum come and get me?"

"She most certainly will not!" laughed Mum, who was coming downstairs. "Your friends are all coming back here after school anyway, aren't they? Well, I'm sure you can wait until then."

"There is a possibility that you might not win you know Frankie," said Dad seriously. "I don't want you building up your hopes too much."

"I know!" I tutted, rolling my eyes, and ran upstairs to get ready for school.

When I got into the playground the others were waiting for me.

"Well?" they asked anxiously.

I shook my head, and watched all their eager smiles turn to major frowns.

"But Dad thinks they might phone us," I explained. "So we'll have to get back to my place as quickly as we can after school this afternoon."

"Yeah, 'cos if the competition is for under-thirteens, they'll probably ring after four o'clock when everybody's finished school, won't they?" said Rosie.

I don't know how we got through that day at school, I really don't. I felt as though I had butterflies in my tummy all day. And it was a Monday too. Mondays are always a little bit harder than the rest of the week, aren't they? It was such a relief to hear the bell at home time.

"Come on, you guys!" I yelled to the others. "Let's get home!"

We gathered all our stuff together and ran home with our bags banging our legs as we went.

"I'm glad you don't live any further away from school," gasped Fliss as we panted up to my front door. "I need a sit down now."

We piled inside and into the kitchen, where Mum was waiting for us.

"Have any letters come for me?" I asked excitedly. "Have there been any phone calls?"

"No and no," Mum replied. "I'm sorry love, maybe you haven't been successful this time. There'll be other competitions."

The others all looked as miserable as I felt.

"They said they'd notify winners before five o'clock," said Fliss, looking at her watch. "It's only ten past four. There's still time for them to ring."

She was right, but none of us felt confident any more.

We were just in the kitchen consoling ourselves with big glasses of Coke and bags of crisps when the phone rang. I threw myself at it and said "Hello" in my poshest voice.

"Hello pumpkin!" said the voice at the other end. It was Dad ringing to say that he would be late home. I mean, what a terrible time to choose to ring up. Didn't he know that we were waiting for an important call?

For the last two weeks time had dragged, but those fifty minutes before five o'clock flashed past.

"Well, I guess that's it!" said Rosie sadly. "It's five o'clock. We'd have heard by now if we'd won. I was so sure that we'd win too."

"I'd like to see the winning entry," said Kenny crossly. "I bet it's a fix and the computer's gone to someone the judges knew."

"They can't do that, can they?" asked Fliss.

"I doubt it," I tried to laugh.

The phone began to ring. My heart jumped but I said, "Let Mum get it, it won't be for us."

"Frankie!" Mum called. "It's for you!"

I ran to take the phone from her and the others crowded round.

"Yes... that's right... really? That's great! I certainly will! Byee!"

I very carefully put the phone down and turned to face the gang.

"Come on Frankie! What's happened?"

The others were so close I couldn't breathe.

"Well…" I began. Suddenly I was so excited I couldn't speak.

"Come on for goodness sake!" Kenny was getting really agitated.

I tried again. "We haven't won first prize…"

"Awww!"

"…but we did get one of the runners-up prizes! The man on the phone said that the judges were very impressed because our club was so original. They'll be sending the CD-Roms to me in the next few days and our Home Page should be on the Net in a week's time! Cool or WHAT!!!"

The others went beserk, whooping and cheering. Mum came in with this huge smile on her face.

"I'm so proud of you!" she cried, pulling us all together in a big hug. "Even if you did have to stay up half the night finishing off your entry!"

"You knew!" I gasped.

"Francesca, my darling," she said, "I know everything. You should know that by now!"

So you see, all our efforts were worth it in the end. The CD-Roms arrived a few days later and they were ace. Everybody came round to my house and helped to unpack the parcel. But as only Rosie and I have computers at the moment, sharing them out was a problem. And Fliss for one was not very happy about that.

"It doesn't seem fair," she moaned. "You two will be able to use them whenever you want and the rest of us won't get a look in."

"What if we promise only to use them when we're all together?" I suggested. "There are six of them so there's one each and one left over."

One of the CD-Roms was called 'Encarta', and it was really great because it was like an encyclopaedia but a lot more exciting.

"This would be really useful at school, you know," Rosie said when we were trying it out.

"Maybe we should donate it to school

then," I suggested. "It would solve the problem of who's going to look after the extra CD-Rom."

"It might even get us back in Mrs Weaver's good books," laughed Kenny. "And it would be one in the eye for the M&Ms!"

When we told Mrs Weaver the next day what we wanted to do, she said that we were really kind and that it was a lovely gesture. And you'll never guess – we ended up doing another assembly! We had to tell the rest of the school about the competition, and then we presented the 'Encarta' CD-Rom to Mrs Poole, our headmistress. It was fantastic. Nothing went wrong and, best of all, the M&Ms were furious about us getting so much attention.

But the most brilliant thing about the whole competition really is our Home Page. Look, I'll show you. Isn't it amazing that we're actually on the Net? I still don't believe it. Look, here are our photographs – don't I look silly in mine? And look at these really cool graphics for our 'Midnight Feast' section. And what about these wicked symbols for our 'Sleepover Games' and 'Spooky Sleepover Stories'? What's totally fab is that there's a section where people who've visited our Home Page can send us messages. We pick up a few every week. I print them out and let the others see them, then we reply to them all. It's great. We've heard from girls as far away as Canada and Norway, which is mind-boggling really. And you remember those email addresses that Lyndz's grandparents sent us? Well, we got in touch with those girls, and now we send messages to them all the time. So thanks to the Internet, we've got loads of new pen-friends.

Oh-oh, can you hear what I hear? Yep, here comes trouble! The others will be knocking down the door if I don't go and let them in. You stay here and make the most of the peace and quiet while you can. It sounds to me as though the others are in the mood for some serious mischief. But hey, that's nothing new, is it!?

Sleepover Girls
on Screen

Fliss perguades the rest of her
friends to come with her when she
goes to audition for a TV
commercial. All starts well with a
great sleepover, but trouble brews
when all the Sleepover pals try for
the same commercial. And Fliss isn't
happy about it at all...

Pack up your sleepover kit
and drop in on the fun!

000675446-5

Sleepover Girls and Friends

Mega news! The Spanish students that the Sleepover Club met on holiday are coming to stay. All sorts of fab activities are planned and the exchange gets off to a great start... until the two groups of friends fall out. What's gone wrong? And what have the M&Ms got to do with it?

Pack up your sleepover kit and have fun in the sun!

000675423-6

Order Form

To order direct from the publishers, just make a list of the titles you want and fill in the form below:

Name ....

Address ....

....

....

Send to: Dept 6, HarperCollins Publishers Ltd, Westerhill Road, Bishopbriggs, Glasgow G64 2QT.

Please enclose a cheque or postal order to the value of the cover price, plus:

UK & BFPO: Add £1.00 for the first book, and 25p per copy for each additional book ordered.

Overseas and Eire: Add £2.95 service charge. Books will be sent by surface mail but quotes for airmail despatch will be given on request.

A 24-hour telephone ordering service is available to holders of Visa, MasterCard, Amex or Switch cards on 0141- 772 2281.

Collins
An *Imprint* of HarperCollins*Publishers*